Meet Zade!

Book One

Bringing Home a New Puppy

By Donna Eliason & Milada Copeland

Illustrated by Heidi Darley

Zade's Family on the Ranch

Zade was born on a sheep ranch
on a cool summer evening.

He has three brothers and two sisters.

His mother and father are very excited to
welcome the puppies into their ranch family.

The ranch is a fun place with
many different animals.

There are sheep, donkeys, ducks, and chickens.

Zade loves being a ranch puppy—so
many fun things to do every day!

On the ranch, every day is a new
adventure for the young pups.

There is so much space to run, and Zade's parents take him on trips to explore the ranch and meet other animals.

Zade has a very loving mother. Every day, she teaches him lessons about life.

His father protects Zade and his siblings when they get too frisky chasing the ducks—ducks can be scary.

All mothers and fathers help their children learn about life. They have a very important job.

Parents are important!

The young pups grow up fast—time flies when every day is full of adventures.

Zade is turning eight weeks old. He is now ready to go to his new human family.

Connor's family is looking for a puppy, and they are coming to meet Zade today.

Zade is happy and curious—meeting new people must be like meeting new animals on the ranch.

The Great Adventure Begins

Zade is a little nervous about saying goodbye to the ranch, to all the animals he knows, and to his dog family.

Living with his human family will be a whole new world for Zade. Puppies are just as nervous about changes as little children.

Zade rides home in a crate in the car because
that is the safest way for a dog to travel.

Zade will now live with his new
family in a house in the city.

He will miss the ranch and his mom and dad.

He is a bit afraid of what his new life will be like.

He is not quite sure what a city is.

Zade and His New Family

Becoming part of a human family is a whole new experience for Zade. He will no longer have fields to run in but will play in a backyard. He will not have the same freedom he had on the ranch—city streets can be a dangerous place.

Zade's new family will have to learn about him and how to take care of him. Zade will also have to learn how to live with his humans.

Zade is hoping his new family will be
kind and will take good care of him.

He hopes he will live in the house with people.

If Zade can't live in the house, he will need shelter from the sun, rain, and cold.

And of course he will need clean water, good food, and a lot of attention from his family.

Zade enjoys spending quality time with his family. Together, they are developing routines so that everyone can get along.

Exercise and play are very important. Every day, Zade looks forward to play time with his family. Playing ball in the backyard or another safe place is always a favorite.

Sometimes they grab a leash and go
on adventures to new places.

Sometimes they learn new tricks and Zade gets treats. Zade really enjoys learning new things.

Connor's Friends Come to Visit

When Connor's friends come over to meet Zade, Connor's mom or dad helps Zade learn how to greet people.

Zade gets so excited to meet new people, he sometimes forgets his manners.

Connor asks his friends to sit quietly in a circle and be still like little mice— that helps Zade to behave.

Remember that some children are afraid of dogs—but some **dogs** are afraid of children.

Connor tells his friends to give Zade a treat by offering it in an open hand under his chin.

Children and dogs have to learn
to be kind to each other.

Sometimes Zade
Gets Too Excited

Zade needs to learn to sit and be
still when he says hi to people.

If Zade jumps on Connor, Connor
hugs himself, looks up at the sky, and
freezes like a statue—just like on the
picture. He doesn't scream or run.

This teaches Zade not to jump on people.

Puppies are curious, like children.
Connor's family is patient with Zade as
he learns the rules of their house.

Things Connor Learns Not to Do:

As Connor plays with Zade, he never hits or kicks him. He learns that he can run and play with Zade, but when he sees a dog he doesn't know, he never runs.

Connor will **never** approach a strange dog—that can be dangerous.

Connor and Zade will become best friends and have many good times together.

Connor Learns
Three Golden Rules:

1. Be kind to animals, they have feelings, too. A new dog is like a new child in school—he wants to make friends and be accepted.

2. Learning proper behavior is as important for Connor as it is for Zade. Connor has to remember not to run and scream around dogs he doesn't know.

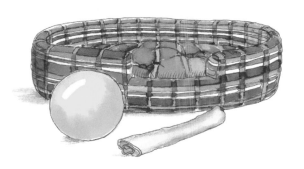

3. Connor will always remember that his job is to take care of his dog. Zade needs food, fresh water, and shelter every day. And Zade needs love and attention—just like Connor does.

Connor is so happy his family got a puppy. Now it will be Connor's job to become responsible and help care for his new best friend, Zade.

About the Authors

Donna Eliason is a professional animal trainer with over forty-five years of experience training horses and dogs. A life-long volunteer with animal rescue groups who's helped find forever homes for countless animals, Donna loves to help people learn to get the most out of the relationship with their dogs. She raised two sons (and many of their friends) on a small working farm, and currently lives in Utah with her husband and four border collies.

Milada Copeland is an animal lover and part-time dog trainer, and a recently retired Army Officer with a professional career in IT security. She has volunteered for animal rescue organizations, focusing on helping dogs settle into their new homes and become good canine citizens. She lives in Utah with her husband and two dogs—a border collie and a herding mixed breed.

About the Illustrator

Heidi Darley is an illustrator, artist, author, and dog lover who lives in Utah with her two standard poodles and family. She has been illustrating for thirty-five years and is excited to combine her two loves: dogs and illustrating.

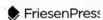
Suite 300 - 990 Fort St
Victoria, BC, V8V 3K2
Canada

www.friesenpress.com

ISBN
978-1-5255-7296-8 (Hardcover)
978-1-5255-7297-5 (Paperback)
978-1-5255-7298-2 (eBook)

1. JUVENILE FICTION, ANIMALS, DOGS

Distributed to the trade by The Ingram Book Company